The rivers and lakes dried up.

There was no water to drink.

Lion, the king of the animals, called a meeting. "We are all thirsty," he said. "We cannot live in this heat. We need water to drink."

The Water Hole

by Amelia Marshall and Can Tugrul

A long time ago, it was very hot

and there was no rain.

The ground dried up.

Nothing could grow.

"I have an idea," Lion went on. "We will dig a water hole. When it rains, the hole will hold the water. Everyone must help to dig." The animals cheered. But Jackal just smiled. He had a different plan.

First Tortoise dug. Then Tiger dug.

Then Baboon dug. All the animals had a go

at digging. They dug and dug, day after day.

Soon they had dug a deep hole.

Then it was Jackal's turn. He looked at the hole.

"It is deep enough now," he said.

"I don't need to dig any deeper. And digging

will make me hot." The animals were angry,

but Jackal wouldn't dig.

Soon, the water hole was finished.

Lion was happy with the animals' work.

"Now we must wait for it to rain," he said.

A few days later, it started to rain.

The hole began to fill with water.

When it got dark, Jackal crept back to

the hole. "I will drink the water first," he said.

Whe he had drunk enough water he climbed

out of the hole and went to sleep in the grass.

In the morning, the animals woke up.

"Now we can drink the water," said Lion.

The animals went to the water hole.

Jackal heard the animals coming. Quickly, he jumped out of the hole filled with water and hid in the long grass.

"Grrr," roared Lion. "The hole is nearly empty.

Someone has been taking the water.

Baboon, you must stay here tonight to catch

the thief."

That night, it rained agin. Baboon sat
by the water hole. But he soon fell asleep.
Jackal came back, carrying a large pot.
Jackal knew Baboon loved honey more
than anything.

"Yum, yum, delicious honey," Jackal sang.
"I don't need any water. I've got
this sweet honey." He sang his song over
and over until Baboon woke up.

"Oh Jackal, please can I have some
of your sweet honey," asked Baboon.
"What will you give me in return?" said Jackal.
"You can drink cool, fresh water from this hole,"
said Baboon.

Jackal kept on eating the honey.

"Oh no Baboon, I don't want water," he said.

"I've got this delicious honey."

"Please give me some," said Baboon." I will let you drink water as many times as you like."

Now Jackal saw his chance.

"There is only a little bit of honey left," he said.

"Here, you can have the pot."

But there was no honey left. The pot was empty.

Jackal put the pot right over Baboon's head.

"Help!" Baboon cried. "Let me out!"

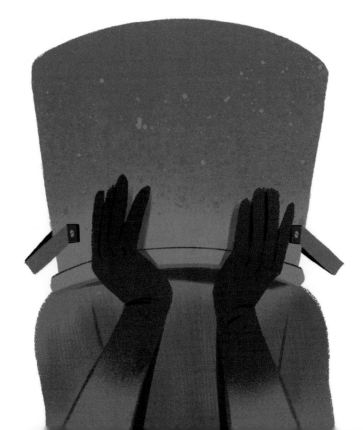

Jackal dived into the water. He swam about and drank as much water as he could. Then he ran off into the night.

Next day, Lion came back to the water hole with the other animals. He found Baboon with a pot on his head.

"So you're the thief!" growled Lion.

"No," cried Baboon, "Jackal tricked me.

"Then you're a fool," said Lion. "I will leave the pot on your head to teach you a lesson."

Story order

Look at these 5 pictures and captions.
Put the pictures in the right order
to retell the story.

1

The water hole is nearly empty.

2

Baboon is left with a pot on his head.

3

Baboon begs Jackal for some honey.

4

The water has all dried up.

5

Jackal wakes up Baboon.

Independent Reading

This series is designed to provide an opportunity for your child to read on their own. These notes are written for you to help your child choose a book and to read it independently.

In school, your child's teacher will often be using reading books which have been banded to support the process of learning to read. Use the book band colour your child is reading in school to help you make a good choice. *The Water Hole* is a good choice for children reading at Gold Band in their classroom to read independently.

The aim of independent reading is to read this book with ease, so that your child enjoys the story and relates it to their own experiences.

About the book

In this world tale from South Africa, crafty Jackal thinks of a way to trick the other animals. He lets them dig a water hole and steals the water while they sleep, leaving the blame with Baboon.

Before reading

Help your child to learn how to make good choices by asking: "Why did you choose this book? Why do you think you will enjoy it?" Look at the cover together and ask: "What do you think the story will be about?" Ask your child to name the animals they can see and think about where the story might be set. Then ask your child to read the title aloud. Ask: "Why do you think the animals need a water hole?" Remind your child that they can sound out the letters to make a word if they get stuck.

Decide together whether your child will read the story independently or read it aloud to you.

During reading

Remind your child of what they know and what they can do independently. If reading aloud, support your child if they hesitate or ask for help by telling the word. If reading to themselves, remind your child that they can come and ask for your help if stuck.

After reading

Support comprehension by asking your child to tell you about the story. Use the story order puzzle to encourage your child to retell the story in the right sequence, in their own words. The correct sequence can be found on the next page.

Help your child think about the messages in the book that go beyond the story and ask: "Why do you think Jackal steals the water when no one is looking? Why does he trick Baboon into thinking there is honey in his pot? Why does Lion blame Baboon for stealing the water instead of Jackal?"

Give your child a chance to respond to the story: "How do you think the other animals felt when they found the water hole nearly empty? Why did Lion ask every animal to help dig the hole? What do you think about how Jackal behaved and how Baboon behaved?"

Extending learning

Help your child predict other possible outcomes of the story by asking: "What do you think would have happened if Baboon had realised that Jackal's pot was empty? Do you think anyone would have realised what Jackal was up to?"

In the classroom, your child's teacher may be teaching different kinds of sentences. There are many examples in this book that you could look at with your child, including statements, exclamations and questions. Find these together and point out how the end punctuation can help us decide what kind of sentence it is.

Franklin Watts
First published in Great Britain in 2022
by Hodder and Stoughton

Series Editors: Jackie Hamley and Melanie Palmer
Development Editors and Series Advisors: Dr Sue Bodman and Glen Franklin
Series Designers: Peter Scoulding and Cathryn Gilbert

A CIP catalogue record for this book is
available from the British Library.

ISBN 978 1 4451 8425 8 (hbk)
ISBN 978 1 4451 8426 5 (pbk)
ISBN 978 1 4451 8506 4 (ebook)
ISBN 978 1 4451 8507 1 (library ebook)

Printed in China

Franklin Watts
An imprint of
Hachette Children's Group
Part of Hodder and Stoughton
Carmelite House
50 Victoria Embankment
London EC4Y 0DZ

An Hachette UK Company
www.hachette.co.uk

www.reading-champion.co.uk

Answer to Story order: 4, 1, 5, 3, 2